Merlin
The Magical Puppy

KING OF THE CASTLE

KEITH LITTLER

CARLTON
BOOKS

Merlin was in big trouble. He peeked out from underneath his blanket.

"It's no use trying to hide," Ernie, the harbour master, said crossly. "Look at this mess. Your home should be your castle, so tidy up in there!"

Merlin sighed. "If I were king of my own castle, I would never have to tidy up. I would be in charge and everyone would have to do what I wanted."

Then Merlin had an idea. He would use his magic collar – if he could remember how it worked.

"I'll try chasing my tail," he barked.

Round and round he went, but nothing happened. Maybe his collar was broken. There was nothing else for it – he would just have to clean up the mess.

"Oh, I wish I could be king of my own castle," he sighed.

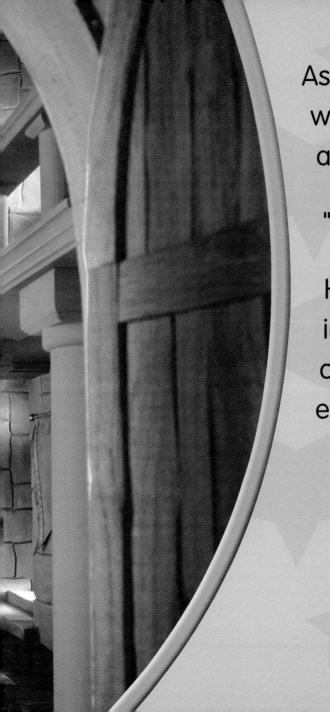

As soon as Merlin said the magic word, "wish", his collar began to glow and sparkle.

"Wow!" he barked.

He was sitting on a very posh throne in a very large castle. In fact, the castle was so large that his bark echoed all around the walls.

"I'm king of the castle," he barked even louder.

"I'm king of the castle...I'm king of the castle...I'm king of the castle..." the walls echoed back at him.

Merlin was enjoying being king. He asked Ernie to make him sausages for tea and then he practised some more echoes.

Mrs Crabtree arrived, looking very worried. "King Merlin, the farmers are upset because it hasn't rained for three weeks and their plants won't grow."

"Oh dear," King Merlin barked.

"And big King Fido from the kingdom next door is going to come and bite you if you don't give him all your sausages and your orange ball by tea-time."

Suddenly Merlin was not enjoying being king any more. He went to his special king-sized kennel to have a think.

"It's not my fault it won't rain," he whined. "I wish it would and I wish that bully King Fido would leave me alone."

As soon as Merlin said the magic word, "wish", his collar began to glow and sparkle.

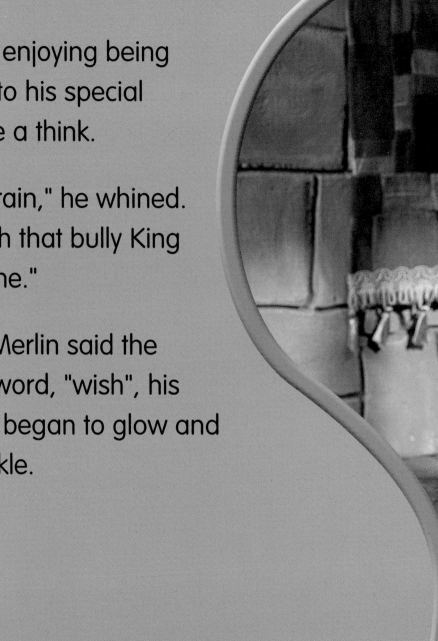

"Goodness me," Ernie shouted happily. "Look out of the window. I do believe it is raining."

Then Mrs Crabtree bustled in. "Good news," she called. "King Fido says he is really sorry if he upset you and he has sent a basket of lovely sausages as a present."

Merlin was overjoyed. "It must have been my magic collar," he barked. "I am so happy I think I will go and make some more echoes!"

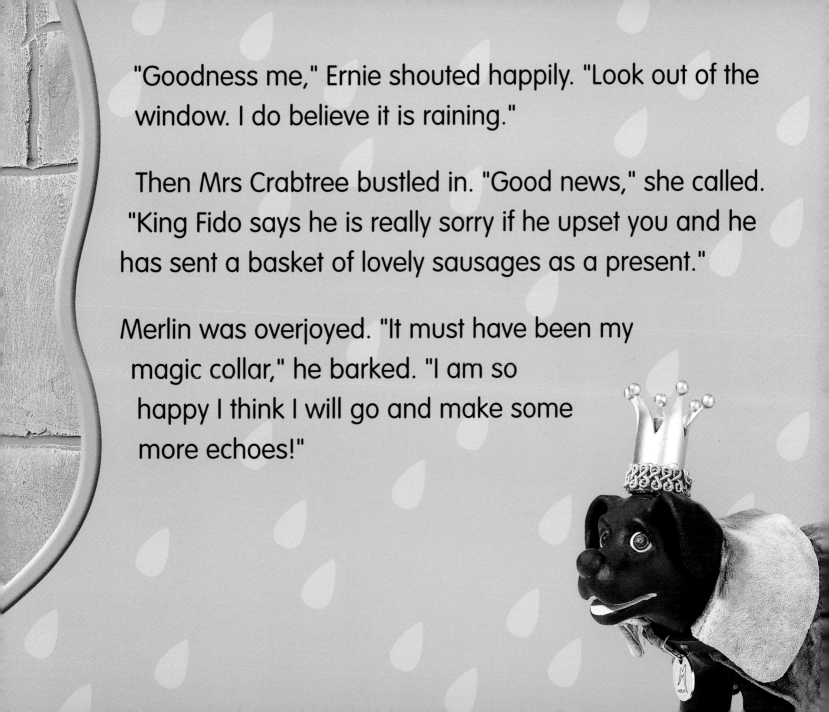

The next day was sunny and hot again. King Merlin went out to explore. On the drawbridge he met Gull.

"Hi, Gull," Merlin barked happily. "Do you want to play?"

"Oh, I can't do that," Gull squawked. "You're the king and I'm only a gull."

Next Merlin bumped into Reg the Hedge.
"Hi, Reg, fancy a game of hide-and-seek?"

"Oh, I can't do that," Reg said. "I'm only a hedgehog. I can't play with a king."

Merlin was bored. It was no fun bossing people about and his friends wouldn't play with him now he was king. He wanted to go home, but he couldn't remember how to make his magic collar work.

Then he met Mrs Crabtree on the drawbridge.

"Ah, King Merlin, there you are," Mrs Crabtree said. "There is to be a royal wedding. Every king must have a queen and yours is waiting for you now."

King Merlin definitely did not want a queen, especially when he saw that his queen was orange with a long tail and whiskers...just like Oscar the cat!